DEATH OF THE MIND

DEATH OF THE MIND

DRAGON APPROVED™ BOOK TWELVE

RAMY VANCE

MICHAEL ANDERLE

DISRUPTIVE IMAGINATION

Thanks to the JIT Readers

Veronica Stephan-Miller
Deb Mader
Kerry Mortimer
Kelly O'Donnell

If we've missed anyone, please let us know!

Editor
The Skyhunter Editing Team

Copyright © 2020 by LMBPN Publishing
Cover Art by Jake @ J Caleb Design
http://jcalebdesign.com / jcalebdesign@gmail.com
Cover copyright © LMBPN Publishing
A Michael Anderle Production

LMBPN Publishing
PMB 196, 2540 South Maryland Pkwy
Las Vegas, NV 89109

First US Edition, June 2020
Version 1.01, October 2020
eBook ISBN: 978-1-64202-948-2
Print ISBN: 978-1-64202-949-9

DEDICATION

To my own little dragons: John and Orla.

—Ramy

To Family, Friends and
Those Who Love
to Read.
May We All Enjoy Grace
to Live the Life We Are
Called.

— Michael

CHAPTER ONE

Alex was in a place she didn't understand.

Only a few minutes ago, she'd gone to sleep, expecting to be overcome by dreams.

And while Alex *was* in a dream, it was unlike anything she'd ever experienced.

She stood behind Vardis, watching him tinkering at a table, the same kind she'd seen in medbays. The sort she vaguely remembered from when she'd had her arm implanted.

There was a coldness in this place, one she was not familiar with. It stretched into her arms, her legs, into every part of her body.

Vardis didn't seem to notice her. He was working on whatever was in front of him on the table.

Alex wanted to get closer, wanted to see what was in front of Vardis, but if she moved, he would know. She didn't know how she possessed that knowledge, but she knew it down to her core. Any movement would make Vardis aware of her existence.

Until moving was necessary, Alex would watch. What she

saw was enough to make her gasp and hope anything except what she was seeing was true.

Seeing wasn't quite the word. It didn't do justice to what was unfolding before her.

The alien was working on a scroll, but the words scrawled on it made no sense to Alex.

Until they did.

Not in the way that words had started to make sense when she was learning braille. There was no clear detailing of ideas, of emotions. Instead, these words called attention to another kind of feeling—one of separation. Each scribble Alex read drew her farther away from the text.

Vardis seemed to be having the same problem, and it was causing him noticeable frustration. The alien slammed his fists on the table, speaking in his own tongue under his breath.

The red shard floated above the texts, the same one Alex and Team Boundless had risked their lives to get. It cast a crimson hue over the scroll and the table.

Frustrated, the alien stood up and tipped the table over as he screamed. The scroll fell, along with everything else, yet the shard remained floating in the air.

Alex jerked away, the sounds of the clattering junk and the scroll hitting the floor ringing in her ear as if a gong had been struck. She yelped in surprise and covered her mouth the moment she heard her own voice.

Vardis turned, his eyes wide and searching.

It was obvious to Alex that he could not see her. Wherever they were, it wasn't a plane that he had any more control over than she did. That was good. This was not a safe situation. Alex was glad that the alien didn't have any noticeable edge over her.

Then the scene changed.

The lab vanished, and Alex was standing on a plain of

blue-green grass that stretched as far as her eye could see. Huts had been built all over the plane and aliens of the same race as Vardis walked to and from the huts.

Few of the beings made eye contact with each other. They seemed to be working hard on something, although Alex could not tell what it was.

Whatever they were occupied with was all-consuming.

Alex could feel it.

Waves and waves of feeling came off them.

Vardis looked at the sky, staring into the purple glow shining from their moon.

Then Alex was back in the lab again, watching Vardis with another scroll. For some reason, she felt like she was less present than she had been previously, as if she were losing her grip on this place.

With that in mind, Alex walked closer to the alien, trying to look over his shoulder and see more details on the document he was working on.

Much like before, the scribbles were not understandable, but not in a way Alex could wrap her head around. But the moment she'd glanced at a few of the indecipherable pencil scratches, she felt her mind rip itself open.

Each individual mark shredded the core of her existence.

Through the pain, she peered at them, trying to understand how to make sense of them.

But there was no sense to be made.

The writing turned black, and the blackness extended beyond the scribbles, finding its way into Alex's chest, and crawling down her spine so each vertebra whispered of its effect.

Alex snapped awake. Or at least, what she thought was awake.

She stood at the edge of a lake that was thick and red like blood. The lake lay beneath two red suns, each beaming down its heat on Alex. She felt like she was going to burst into flames. The feeling eased, and the liquid boiled at her feet.

Wherever she was made no sense. It was worse than when she'd been in the Dark One's mind. At least there had been some kind of focus in that situation. This felt like walking around in the head of a madman.

And if Alex's assumptions were correct, this was just the beginning. Alex wondered what level of Vardis' mind this was. In any case, she had to figure out how to get out.

As she stared at the liquid's surface, she could see images moving back and forth as if they were fish. Some of the images were of Vardis, and others were too blurry for Alex to see.

Curiosity got the better of her and she plunged her hand into the liquid, surprised it didn't burn her skin. She grasped one of the images of Vardis and tried to pull it out.

The memory resisted moving past the surface of the water as if it had turned solid. "Memories," Alex muttered to herself. "Those must be memories."

That made the most sense. Vardis had told Alex they were connected psychically. The extent of the connection hadn't been explained, but Alex could see it was strong enough to drag her from her dreams into Vardis' mind.

Which meant the alien, in all likelihood, had no idea she was walking around in his subconscious.

The lab. There had been something important in the lab, something about the scrolls Vardis was working on.

Alex felt like she could make sense of the messages if she were only able to get closer. All she had to do was navigate through Vardis' dreams.

Maybe there was something in them that would springboard Alex to that particular memory.

Alex plunged her hands back into the red liquid before

her as the sky darkened with clouds. All around her, houses began to spring up as if they were flowers, building themselves in a series of ornate circles. The structures were circular and diminutive.

As Alex fished around, she tried to focus on what she'd seen when she'd first entered the dream. Vardis had been standing over some kind of table. The surrounding details were fuzzy, but Alex had the feeling that the room was in a science department or something like that, or maybe a medbay. She was certain the memory was from this planet.

Something bit Alex's hand, and she quickly pulled it back and held it to her chest. Along with her hand came a memory, which evaporated as soon as it left the water.

As the memory around Alex started to shift and crumble, the red suns cracking down the middle, and the earth trembling, she peered into the lake.

She could see a child's version of Vardis' face floating to the top of the water, its eyes black and empty—a curled fetus, tail hugging its body.

As Alex tried to peer more closely, the liquid began to drain from the lake. Walls shot up out of the ground, separating hallway from hallway until Alex found herself in a military base not too different from the Nest, although more technologically advanced.

Aliens who looked like Vardis were running down the corridor, rushing past Alex without noticing her.

Either these memory people couldn't see her, or they didn't think there was anything strange about her. Either way, she was free to move about as she liked.

Alex followed the aliens, running to keep up with them and appreciating that stamina didn't matter in a dream.

They stopped at a door, one of them reaching out and resting his hand on a panel at the side. The door slid open, and the aliens stepped in.

Alex slipped into the room behind them.

The aliens walked farther into the room, then stopped and talked among themselves. Vardis stood in the distance, hunched over a table.

He was looking at the same scroll as before, and she could see the shard next to his hand.

Alex got closer to the aliens, placing her head between the two of them as they spoke. After a few seconds, she could understand them—not the words, more like pictures against the back of her head, which explained everything and more.

The aliens were afraid.

They were terrified of whatever Vardis had created. They had heard about it and been told about his ambitions, but they hadn't thought it could be done.

The kin were not to be trusted.

It was as simple as that. There had never been anything more terrifying and horrible than the kin—until the Dark One came.

Alex wasn't certain what the kin were. Vardis had given her a brief explanation, but the way these aliens were acting made it seem as if the beasts were something much more complex than Vardis had alluded to.

And much more dangerous.

The two aliens flanking her discussed whether to kill Vardis right there. If he succeeded in his experiments, there was no telling how dangerous the kin might be. But then, he was trying to create a weapon to defeat the Dark One. Maybe they just weren't opening their eyes wide enough.

Vardis turned, and Alex leaped out of his line of sight. He didn't seem to notice her anyway. He was too busy crying. "The Dark One will destroy all of us. You know that, don't you?" Vardis whimpered to his colleagues. "If we don't find a way to kill him, he'll wipe out everything in the universe."

One of the aliens stepped forward to reason with the

scientist. "Yes, but the kin? Given everything they've destroyed, you would inflict that pain on our world again?"

As the aliens spoke, Alex snuck to the table, standing on the opposite side of it as Vardis talked. Alex looked down at the manuscript next to the shard. She didn't understand what it said in a literal sense, but she was hit with all the emotions and disjointed thoughts that Vardis must have had about it.

There would be time to make sense of it later. Somehow, she knew it would be easier after she woke up from Vardis' dream. *And how long is that going to take?* she thought.

As Alex turned, preparing to leave, Vardis turned and saw her. The tone in the dream instantly changed. It was like all of the heat and air in the room had been sucked out.

Vardis screamed, pointing at Alex, sending her flying through the wall as the construct of the dream started to break down around her. For a moment, she flew through stars, then through walls, then through the crevices of her own mind. *Guess he knows I'm here,* Alex thought to herself. *Wonder how long it's going to take for him to find me.*

CHAPTER TWO

Alex was flying through the blackness, watching Vardis racing toward her. For some reason, she wasn't concerned. The universe around her stretched too far and Vardis was so distant. Alex realized there was probably something in play that was keeping her from being overwhelmed by a sense of danger.

She knew this was a dangerous situation. Vardis' mind would be a powerful place. But it looked as if he were just as confused by what was happening as Alex was. Maybe if he had been better prepared, he would have been able to muster a stronger attack.

For the time being, Alex was going to use this surprise to her advantage. She wasn't sure if she could pull herself out of Vardis' dream, leaving him to wake up confused, thinking that he'd been dreaming about the human. It wasn't like Alex had gone out of her way to sneak into the alien's dreams.

Besides, once she was out, she knew she would be able to understand the manuscript Vardis had been working on.

The blackness around her felt like a shrine. It was getting

deeper and deeper as Vardis was getting further and further away. The alien couldn't catch up with Alex.

Alex closed her eyes, trying to wretch herself from Vardis' dream. It wasn't happening. She was still stuck in the alien's dreams.

Vardis was nowhere to be seen. Alex figured if she couldn't get herself out of Vardis' dreams, then she might as well explore and see what else she could find. The process shouldn't have been much harder than pulling one of Vardis' memories from the pond.

The problem was Alex didn't know where to start. She knew that the blackness she was floating through probably meant something, but she had no idea. The book on dream interpretation she'd been reading seemed very far away, the ideas foreign and incomprehensible.

Then the blackness receded as if Vardis' mind had heard Alex's complaints about not understanding anything.

Alex was no longer in the dark of Vardis' mind. He must have slipped deeper into sleep, conjuring a new place for Alex to wander through. She was back on the planet with the red suns. It must have been Vardis' home planet.

She was in a field much like the one she'd seen earlier. But there were no buildings this time, no lake. Instead, a place in the field where the grass had been cut down low. Geometric patterns had been carved into the dirt, and the grooves filled with a red kind of liquid.

Alex walked up to the bald spot in the grass and stared at the patterns. They made sense, but only in the same kind of primitive way that reading over Vardis' shoulders had. Alex gathered what was important. This was a bad place, and it was a place of her own creation.

She looked down at her hands. They were covered in blood, and when she touched her forehead, she felt the blood there as well. Alex looked sideways and saw there were aliens standing next to her. All of them with blood on their hands and foreheads.

The three aliens gathered around the patterns in the dirt, motioning for Alex to follow them. She did as she was told. There was nothing else to do. She had to know what was happening.

The four of them all bowed their heads and closed their eyes before humming came from them.

Dread gripped Alex. They were calling something, something that should never be called. Their voices cast into the darkness, going forth into a place that touched the brink of Alex's mind, even here, deep within Vardis' dream.

This was a memory and yet so much more. A deep blooded connection that ran through Vardis and could never be forgotten. How he had come to this knowledge, Alex did not know. But it extended beyond the simple framework of waking and sleeping.

The aliens stared up into the sky as they sang softly, Alex singing along with them, uncertain of how she knew the song but certain she'd never forget.

The sky darkened, clouds gathering and lightning casting bright flashes of brightness throughout the field.

A creature loomed in the hefty weight of the clouds, a creature so large that it took up the entire sky, its bright eyes, thousands upon millions of them staring out from the dark, searching and searching until they found what they were looking for.

Alex could feel the creature's eyes rolling over her body, sliding into every pore, cutting her mind open from the inside. She would have screamed if she remembered how. But that was not why she was here. That wasn't why any of them were here.

The aliens at her side weren't bothered by the unknowable creature up above. They regarded it with the coolness of scientists. They were busy taking notes, occasionally looking up at the sky and commenting on what they saw.

Then one of the aliens pulled a red shard from a bag and placed it in the middle of the patterns drawn into the ground.

The creature above shrieked as a bright light peeled through the sky, turning everything white for a second. A red tornado shot up from the shard, sucking in all of the eyes that peered down on the aliens and Alex, yanking them from their celestial place, and shoving them into the red shard in the middle of the balding spot of the field.

Once the sky returned to normal, the three aliens spoke among themselves, motioning to Alex to come closer and check out the shard. Alex could see billions of eyes staring out at her from the shard.

One of the aliens held the shard out to Alex. "Eaters of worlds," the alien said slowly. "Caught easily enough. We should hold on to this one just in case we have to use it."

Then the scene changed.

Alex was standing in a laboratory. Vardis was there, but he was in a meeting with a handful of aliens of his kind. They were seated at a table, poring over notes. The red shard was in the middle of the table.

Vardis stood and cleared his throat. He pointed to a screen playing behind him. But it wasn't quite a screen. It looked as if the screen were floating in the air but had no tangible existence. "As you can see from the projection, we could use the Old One as a weapon. It is a creature, just like any other. Matter and material. A nearly infinite source of matter. By using the changes I want to implement to its holding shard, we could create completely new creatures from the Old One. An infinite army."

The aliens talked back and forth with each other, trying to come to a consensus. Alex could feel the tension in the room and she hid in the back, trying to keep from being seen by the scientist. She wanted to see how this all played out.

One of the aliens stood, anger radiating from his body. "You realize what you're saying, don't you? How much energy that would take? It could—"

Vardis raised his hand to silence the alien. "Drain an entire planet of its energy. Yes. We would, in essence, be using a devourer to stop another devourer. The only difference is that ours will remain chained up. A war is not won without sacrifice."

Another of the aliens jumped to his feet. "You're insane!"

The alien closest to Vardis stood and clapped his hand on Vardis' shoulder. "No, he's a genius! Who else would have thought this up? It's all theoretical anyway. But it's good to know that we have the possibility. An Elder One against the Dark One. Genius, pure genius."

Vardis didn't look happy with the praise. He was staring at the red shard, its hue reflected in the darkness of his eyes.

One of the aliens began speaking, but all his words came out backward. He climbed onto the table and started dancing, his legs jerking back and forth while he bopped up and down, occasionally pumping his hands.

Vardis rubbed his brow as if he were embarrassed for the alien on the table. "Please, Devardra, not now. I'm trying to study."

The alien stopped, his head tilting back as he leaned back, his spine snapping as his hands touched the table. "But you never want to dance with me!"

The table shattered into a thousand pieces as the walls grew soft and hairy and then long and silky, draining down into the floor as Vardis paced back and forth, finally reaching out and grabbing the shard and retreating away from the table as the other alien continued to dance upon the table like some mad imp.

Alex blinked, and everything was different.

She was standing in a city, not so different from the archival footage she'd seen of a mission that had taken place in an area of Middang3ard that had been taken over by the Dark One. The buildings stretched high into the sky.

The tech in the city was amazing. Every building was sleek and seemed to have been poured from a material Alex had yet to see. But the streets were empty.

No, that wasn't right. They weren't empty. Dead bodies were everywhere.

In the cars. In the buildings. Piled high in the fountain. Blood was flowing.

Vardis was kneeling down in front of a fountain filled with the bodies of his people. He was weeping quietly. The shard was in his hand.

Alex would never have thought Vardis had been capable of this.

The shard and Vardis' hand were covered in blood. As Alex got closer, she could see the faces of the aliens in the fountain. She had to step over the bodies of dozens of other aliens just to get close.

Anger welled up in Alex. This was what Vardis was planning on doing to her world? To Middang3ard? How could he do this to a whole planet again? "You're not doing this to my world!" Alex shouted.

Vardis jumped up, clutching the shard to his chest. "Do what? I didn't do this. I would never do this." He looked around at the damage, at the bodies lining the streets, their eyes upturned to the sky, the bloodstains that seemed to be everywhere. "*He* did this."

Vardis stumped forward, his eyes wide and frantic. He didn't let go of the shard, but with his free hand, he pointed at the sky. "He did it." Then Vardis fell to his knees, weeping louder than before. "I'm not letting it happen again. Never again."

The alien slashed out with his hand, sending a telekinetic blast at Alex. It hit her square in the chest, sending her flying through the air.

Vardis was up again, his feet slightly levitating off the ground as he floated toward Alex. "He will never do this again."

CHAPTER THREE

A lex and Vardis stared each other down as they began to circle each other. She wasn't sure what kind of weapons were going to be available to her.

This was a dream, after all. And one that wasn't of her creation.

If Vardis was able to pull all of this out of his memory without realizing it, what was going to keep him from being able to handicap Alex?

But Alex was still partially in her mind too.

She wasn't a passive part of this dream, being acted upon in ways over which she had no control. Originally, she'd been interested in what Vardis had been reading in the lab. Now she knew what it was about but had an even larger concept of what Vardis was capable of causing.

Then a thought crossed Alex's mind. What if this wasn't even him? Not Vardis as she had been used to him, aware and active. These could just be memories he was living through. There was a chance he wasn't even aware she was in his dreams.

Alex raised her hand. "Wait, what are you not going to let happen again?"

Vardis surged forward, ignoring her question. Alex felt herself lifting into the air. Guess Vardis was aware enough to fight.

Alex went flying again, caught in the throes of Vardis' psychic attack. It was a shame she wasn't a telekinetic as well. *Wait,* Alex thought. *I wasn't telepathic until I met Chine, and I wasn't that strong a telepath until Vardis connected me with him.*

She pushed aside any thoughts of what she was or wasn't capable of. Besides, this was a dream. Alex had done stranger things in them.

As she flew through the air, Alex twisted around to see Vardis heading toward her. She concentrated, tried to feel the flow of energy around her—the physical manifestation of Vardis' will. Then she pushed out with her own.

Alex didn't stop, but she slowed down. She pushed again, imagining a giant hand around her body, prying Vardis' grip off her.

Suddenly, Alex hit the floor.

Vardis stopped in his tracks. "How did you do that?"

Alex reached out to draw her scythe, then noticed she wasn't wearing her anchor. Maybe it didn't matter. She imagined a psychic scythe and flicked it into existence. "I'm a quick learner."

Vardis raised his hand, a ball of telekinetic energy forming in his palm. "Maybe too quick for your own good." He threw it.

Alex flung up her hand, imagining a shield around her body.

The ball exploded, pushing Alex into the floor. She had almost felt the force of the attack. The shield had absorbed a lot, but she was not nearly as strong as Vardis was, not yet at least. She'd have to make sure not to rely on one trick.

Alex shook off the attack and sprinted forward, holding her scythe out, and leaped, landing behind Vardis. When she swung her scythe, the alien stepped out of the way, raised his hand, and shot a blast at Alex, who was barely able to throw up a shield in time.

The two stood there toe to toe, blasting each other. Vardis was easily able to deflect Alex's attacks. Her attempts weren't doing much either. Vardis easily waved them away. *More than one trick,* Alex thought to herself before dropping to one knee fast and slicing at Vardis' legs.

The scythe cut through Vardis' body, separating his ankle from his leg. He screamed in pain as he cupped his hands and sent a telepathic blast at Alex.

The blast hit hard, knocking Alex off her feet.

Vardis screamed as the world around him began to break apart again.

Alex thought she was ready for it this time. She held up her hand, trying to deflect the next attack.

The world slanted, and when it righted itself, Alex was on an operating table.

Vardis stood over her, holding a saw and wearing a nurse's smock. "We're going to cut you up!" He slammed the saw into Alex's chest.

Alex screamed in pain as she felt the saw tearing through her skin, cutting through her sternum. Instinctively, she raised her hand and sent out a blast that threw Vardis across the room.

When Alex looked down at her chest, it was bleeding but not enough to kill her. A couple of seconds more, and Alex would have been dead on the table. If this were real life, this wound would have killed her. Maybe it was better not to think about it too much.

Vardis came flying from the side of the room, two saws in hand. He tackled Alex, sending her into the wall, and the two of them struggled to get to each other as the room rotated.

Alex flung a psychic blast that knocked Vardis off of her. He slashed at her back as they scrambled to get to their feet. She took a step forward and fell into a huge puddle.

Vardis stood above her. He raised his hands and Alex floated out of the water, enclosed in a giant bubble. She grasped her throat, trying to breathe before pulling out her scythe and slicing through the bubble. "Are you planning to destroy our world like you did your own?"

Vardis said nothing. He merely flipped Alex over and chopped her in the back of the neck. He was faster than she was here. Made sense. It was Vardis' dream. He had the home team advantage.

Alex was going to have to figure something out quickly.

Chine, that was it! The dragon was in the waking world, but despite that, his connection with Alex was strong. Maybe even stronger now that Alex had started to come into her own as a telepath.

Alex reached out to the dragon, focusing her thoughts and directing them toward him. The gist of the sentiment was, "Help!" As she sent her telepathic SOS, she flipped back onto her feet, pulled the psychic scythe out again, and slashed at Vardis, forcing the alien back.

He stumbled away from Alex. It was an opening and Alex took it, rushing forward and slicing at Vardis again, forcing him to retreat as he tossed up a psychic shield. Alex didn't relent. She threw attack after attack at him until the alien raised his hands and screamed, sending Alex flying as the structure of the dream started to shift again.

This time Alex concentrated on where she wanted to go. She imagined the lab where she'd first seen Vardis hunched over a scroll, but this time, Alex made sure he wasn't there.

The open sky transformed into the walls of the lab, and

Alex was now standing in front of the table on which the scroll lay open. Vardis was nowhere to be seen.

Alex started reading. She had no idea what the scribbles on the page said, but she knew the meaning behind them. They were notes on the shard, on how it operated and how to destroy it. Alex was certain she'd remember all this once she got out of the dream. She'd be able to piece it together in the real world.

"What are you doing?"

Alex spun to see Vardis standing on the threshold of the lab. He raised his hands and powered up another psychic blast.

Before he could fire, the walls of the lab burst open, sending debris everywhere as Chine forced his way in, ether fire spouting of out his mouth as the rider ran to him.

Vardis projected a shield, blocking the fire.

Alex climbed onto her dragon's back. "We need to get out of here! How do we do that?"

Chine's eyes narrowed on Vardis. "It is his dream. We must wake him up." With that, Chine barreled toward Vardis and snatched the alien and his shield in his mouth.

Alex leaped off Chine's back and landed on his snout. She pulled out her scythe and started to hack at the shield the alien was trembling behind.

The shield burst like a balloon, and Vardis was suspended in the air for a second before he was consumed by the ether flames Chine fired.

Vardis screamed in rage and pain as he launched one more attack at Alex, a sort of psychic buzz saw. The blast hit her in the shoulder, and she toppled off the dragon's back as she gripped her wound.

Alex hit the floor hard. She tried to get up, but she was tangled in something. She wiped her hair out of her face and saw that she was in her bedroom, on the floor, wrapped in her blankets. That was interesting.

When Alex finally made it out of her blankets, she winced in pain. She took off her shirt and saw she was bleeding from cuts on her chest and her shoulder. They weren't as deep as they had been in the dream, but they were substantial.

Alex wondered if Vardis was going to be taking home any scars.

CHAPTER FOUR

Alex's alarm went off, blaring loudly. She grabbed her dragon anchor and slipped it over her wrist as she stood. The pain in her chest and shoulder immediately got worse. Even though they were only surface wounds, they hurt as badly as they had when she was in Vardis' dream.

She looked down at the wound across her sternum before gingerly touching it. There was a lot of blood. It was going to need to be taken care of before she left for her pickup to return to Middang3ard. There was no way her parents were going to let her out of the house if she was bleeding through her clothes.

Alex grabbed a robe from her closet and peeked out of her bedroom. No one was in the hall. She made a run for the bathroom across from her room and locked the door.

The medicine cabinet was always overstocked. Her father was something of a germaphobe and her mother was a worrier, always thinking of the worst-case scenario. That meant they not only had tons of antiseptic but also a robust first aid kit that would put most military medical units to shame.

Alex found the kit under the sink. The antiseptics were in the medicine cabinet.

Luckily, Alex had paid close attention to her classes that dealt with wounds in the field. The armor she wore while riding protected her from most weapon and plasma attacks, but there was only so far armor could go. Alex had found that out firsthand when her arm had been taken off.

The class had offered detailed explanations of how to deal with a variety of combat wounds, accompanied by a demo on a lifelike prosthetic. Alex had practiced more than anyone else after losing her arm.

Cuts and gashes had been the first level of injury they'd studied. Needless to say, Alex had practiced enough that disinfecting her wounds and dressing them herself wasn't going to be a problem. That didn't mean it wasn't going to hurt.

She took a deep breath as she prepared herself for the sting of the alcohol, then tossed it on her chest and her shoulder, wincing and inhaling sharply as the wounds exploded in red pain. Then she dabbed them with one of the towels hanging from the sink before rinsing them again.

Once Alex was satisfied the wounds were clean, she opened the first aid kit and located a pair of latex gloves, a needle, and some thread. She put on the gloves and started with her shoulder, trying to ignore the pain and focus on the needle going in and out of her skin. She drew the thread tight and tied off the sutures. That was the easier one.

Next, she got started on her chest, following the same process, albeit slower than before, stopping from time to time to catch her breath before dousing the gash with more disinfectant and starting to sew again. It took her about thirty minutes; her instructors would have been impressed. The wounds had been closed very nicely. She could get the stitches removed on the base in a few days.

Then Alex bandaged herself, making sure to use enough gauze that if the wounds started bleeding again, the blood wouldn't make it through the fabric of her shirt. Once she was done, she brushed her teeth and wiped herself down.

She went back to her bedroom, got dressed, and checked through the regular messages on her anchor. Apparently, there was a problem at the base, and the chauffeur who was to have picked Alex up wasn't going to make it. She was going to have to walk to the meeting point designated by the base. Alex groaned in irritation. Napping in the back of a car sounded great. Putting strain on her body sounded terrible.

But she was also looking to see if there had been any updates about anything happening at the base. She still wasn't certain if Vardis had been aware that she'd been in his dream. She only vaguely remembered what had happened.

Until it all hit, rushing back at her with the force of a tidal wave. Alex remembered everything: the fights, the shifting memories, all of it. Most importantly, Alex remembered what she'd read on Vardis' notes.

The weapon had never been used.

All the destruction Alex had seen in Vardis' memories had been done by the Dark One's forces. That was only the beginning of what the Dark One was capable of.

Alex had heard of the situation on the gnomish planet. It didn't seem to be nearly as bad as what Vardis' people had experienced. With Middang3ard, the Dark One seemed more interested in absorbing and reprogramming the different races of the nine realms. This was the first time Alex had seen the flat-out destruction the Dark One was capable of.

Further, Alex had not expected the Dark One to be so ruthless. She had assumed there was meaning or desire behind the havoc he wreaked, but having seen streets full of dead people, she wondered if the Dark One was a psychopath with dimensional powers. No rational creature would delight in dealing out that much destruction.

Another thing Alex remembered was that the notes had included a way to stop the weapon.

Yet that was an odd memory.

She couldn't think of how to turn off the weapon, but much like in the dream, she was certain she would know what to do when the time came.

That left Alex feeling unprepared and uncomfortable. She didn't want to trust a vague notion, but there was nothing else she could do. Most of what she'd read she remembered verbatim, even though she didn't understand the alien language. Why was that part hidden from her?

Just because no one in Boundless had messaged Alex about anything happening at the base didn't mean Vardis wasn't suspicious. She messaged each team member individually, asking if they had seen or spoken with the alien.

Jollies was the first to reply. She let Alex know she and Vardis had eaten breakfast together, and there didn't seem to be anything wrong. He was excited to get back to Middang3ard, implement the weapon, and finally get rid of the Dark One.

Alex carefully phrased her response, making sure not to give the pixie anything to worry about. Then she got dressed and went downstairs.

Both of Alex's parents were in the kitchen, working on breakfast together. They looked up when they saw her, their faces grim for a moment before they each forced a smile. "You sleep okay?" Claire asked as Alex took a seat at the kitchen nook.

Alex shuffled the newspapers that were on the counter. "Yeah, why?"

"We heard you screaming last night. A lot."

George came over and took a seat next to Alex. He

hugged her tightly. "You know you can talk to us, right? We know everything you're going through is kind of a lot. We're always here for you."

Alex caught her father looking at her robotic hand. She covered it with her sweater and took a sip of the orange juice in front of her. "Yeah, I know. There's not much to talk about. We're getting closer to destroying the Dark One, and once that's done, life goes back to normal."

"Is it dangerous? What you have to do?"

Alex thought about telling her parents the truth. Maybe this was the time, or maybe there would never be a time. Just because her parents were somewhat familiar with the workings of Middang3ard due to VR, it didn't mean they were ready to deal with the rest of her life.

It hurt that she was hiding something from them, but she knew it was best. The worries that her parents could dream up in their heads were nothing compared to what Alex had to face daily. Best to leave them to their own devices.

Alex put on her best convincing smile. "Nope. This is the easiest thing I'll ever do. And before you know it, the war will be over."

George sighed with relief as Claire motioned for him to come back to the stove to give her a hand.

The rest of the morning was the most normal Alex had had for quite some time. She ate and joked with her parents as if there were no war. It felt like she'd never left, and she was starting to wish she didn't have to.

When Alex had first gone to Middang3ard, it was to ride a dragon. Sure, she knew there was a war going on and had seen a bit of what it had consisted of, but it wasn't the draw.

She couldn't believe how naïve she'd been only a couple of months ago. She felt like a completely different person now. She had a whole new set of priorities, worrying about her team and the rest of the nine realms. Riding was incidental to fighting.

When they finished the meal, Alex helped clean up and do the dishes. No one talked much. It was as if the illusion of normalcy was over. Once the dishes were done, Alex was going off to continue fighting a war.

Afterward, Alex drifted into the living room, trying to memorize each detail. She'd grown up in this house and had only seen it once or twice. She didn't want to forget how it looked.

Claire came up behind Alex and wrapped her arms around her daughter. "We love you, and we're very proud of you."

Alex squeezed her mom's hand and said, "I know. I love you too."

George came over and joined the hug. They stood holding each other for some time in silence, each of them no doubt trying to dream up scenarios where Alex came back home to them, unharmed and happy.

But the rider knew those were only hopes. She would have to make sure they came true. Otherwise, she was going to leave behind two broken parents in the chaos the realms would be in. She felt like she'd be more responsible for that pain than anyone else.

CHAPTER FIVE

Alex headed for the military base. The coordinates had been loaded onto her dragon anchor, and it wasn't too far away. She was surprised she'd never heard there was a military base so close to her house, but it made sense.

Neither of her parents would have cared, and a few months ago, she wouldn't have either.

The walk was interesting. Alex had only seen her neighborhood from a car, speeding off to her first mission.

She'd never walked down the street in a leisurely fashion and looked around. Simple things like that never failed to impress her.

Much of her life now was insane. She rarely got to stop and appreciate the small miracle of being able to see. For much of her life, she had existed in darkness, but here was a world full of light and beauty. It was something she needed to stop and appreciate more.

Alex took her time, intentionally ignoring the GPS directions her anchor gave that would have had her walking along main streets. She favored the smaller, more pleasant streets.

A cottage covered in pink and blue wildflowers like

something out of a fairytale was extremely out of place in the suburban landscape.

An old man was sitting on the porch, playing fetch with his dog. The man was too old to stand to retrieve the ball from his dog, and the dog was too young to care.

Two young lovers were sitting in a park, enjoying a picnic and speaking quietly to each other.

When Alex saw those last two, her heart clenched. It had only been a day or two ago that she and Jim had been out on a picnic together. That had ended quickly enough. Since then, she'd hardly had a moment to share a word with him. She knew he understood. He was just as caught up in everything as she was.

She wanted to be out on a date with Jim right now. To be anywhere with him, doing anything other than the mission on hand. Something about this felt much heavier than anything she'd faced to date. Sitting down in quiet peace next to Jim would have been vastly preferable.

There would be time for that once the Dark One was defeated. They could go on to their normal lives. But what if there wasn't a life for Jim and Alex after this? What if they'd only been brought together by the sheer ludicrousness of the war and, when it was over, they had nothing left? There had hardly been time to get to know each other in the past month.

Or maybe they knew each other better than Alex would admit. They'd been fighting alongside each other for months, in VR and in real life. They'd seen parts of each other that Alex didn't even know existed within her.

Alex realized she'd stopped walking and was staring at the couple, who only now noticed her. She looked down at her anchor and continued walking.

Now that the war could come to an end, Alex entertained what life might be like after the Dark One was taken care of.

Was she going to go back to being homeschooled?

She couldn't think of anything more anticlimactic, but that was what happened to everyone after a war.

Once WWII was over, her grandfather had come back to the States and started working at a tire shop.

Part of Alex felt guilty for resenting this idea already. She didn't want to go back to living a normal life after experiencing what it was like to be a hero. That felt selfish, but Alex couldn't ignore it. She'd found out she was a warrior. What would she do after the fight was over?

Alex remembered the Dark One's words and promises.

He had said that he could make her and all of Boundless rulers of this world. And other worlds, too.

Ruling didn't appeal to Alex, but the idea of continuing to be somebody who mattered stuck in her mind. She didn't want to go back to being nobody.

Yeah, trust the words of a madman, Alex thought.

She didn't know why she was letting herself entertain the idea. A bargain with the Dark One would be selling her soul, and she couldn't really think that was an option after the atrocities she'd seen him commit.

Yet there was the fear.

Alex knew she had to destroy the weapon.

She knew what it was capable of doing to the world, to the nine realms.

Yet, if she destroyed the weapon, she'd be doing what the Dark One wanted. There had to be a way to destroy him along with the weapon.

As Alex turned the corner, she realized she was not only thinking in circles but also walking in them. She'd seen Vardis' notes and sorted through his memories. If the weapon was used, it would be catastrophic. Unfortunately, nothing was ever that easy.

Alex needed someone to talk this through with, but all of

her options seemed terrible. She focused her thoughts toward Chine. *Hey, buddy, you there?*

A rush of Chine's emotions hit Alex as he answered, *Dustling, I have been worried about you since the dream. Are you all right?*

She knew Chine cared enough about her to worry, but it still warmed Alex's heart. It was the same with her parents. *Yeah, I'm okay. Still a little shook up about everything that happened. It was a lot to take in.*

Your telepathy has grown so strong. I wouldn't have thought you were skilled enough to project yourself into Vardis' dreams, let alone call me into them as well.

What do you mean, call you into them? I just sent a message.

An image of Chine smiling the way only dragons could flashed through Alex's mind. *No, you did more than call me. You drew me from my own dreams into a dream space you and Vardis shared. Even among dragons, only our oldest and most skilled are capable of supporting a space with that many dreamers. I still am a little impressed.*

Alex found she was in a park. She must have lost track of where she was going. Instead of setting out again, she walked over to a bench and took a seat. *Do you think he knew we were in there? In his dreams?*

Chine took a moment to answer. *That is a good question. Generally, no, he shouldn't have. What you fought within those dreams was not Vardis. It was a projection of his unconscious mind. But that is how it works for dragons and the rest of the sentients in the nine realms. Vardis is from a different dimension, so his mind might work differently than ours.*

Alex realized the park she was sitting in was the same park in which she'd been watching the couple. They were staring at her now. She thought it best to start moving again. *Do you know what he's up to? Vardis?*

He has hidden his thoughts and feelings from me since he

arrived at the Nest. I didn't think it was suspicious at the time because it is a habit all telepaths have when meeting new people, but his defenses are high. I've never been certain of where he is or what he is doing.

Alex checked her GPS again and headed in the direction of the military base. She still had at least another half an hour to walk.

It dawned her that this was the longest time she'd been alone in a while. It was the longest she'd walked by herself without one of her parents nearby.

You ever get tired of always being around people? she asked Chine.

He chuckled, a rich and hearty sound. *Why would you ask that?*

I don't know. I figured you might feel like me sometimes—always having to do things for other people, never getting a moment to yourself. When you do, it's like you can't even enjoy it.

My perspective might be different from yours. Dragons, for most of our lives, are very social. It isn't until we are older and near the end of our lives that we live in solitude, usually away from the dragon realms, doing everything in our power to keep others from finding where our enclave is. It is those dragons, the elders who choose to spend time all alone, who fill the legends and lore of humans.

So, you wish you were around more dragons?

Chine chuckled again, the warmth absent this time and a hint of bitterness taking its place. *I have made peace with the sacrifices that must be made until the Dark One is defeated, but yes. Yes, I am often lonely. It is good to be with the dragons from the Boundless, but my family and friends are growing old without me. There are few things that can ease that pain.*

Alex thought about what he had said, taking her time. The dragon was right; it was a different perspective.

She enjoyed the closeness she was developing with the

members of her team. They were as tightly knit as family, and she loved that.

Alex crossed the street, running to make it before the light changed. She was almost at the base.

There was a sigh in her mind, followed by Chine's voice. *Dustling, you are going to have to make the most important decision of your life soon.*

Alex stopped and looked at the sun above her. Clouds were starting to gather, blocking the light. *You mean, destroying the shard?*

The dragon's face shone in front of Alex for a second. *Only you know what you've learned. Those around you—your family, the Boundless, the Nest—will understand your decision, whatever it is. They trust you. Perhaps you should have faith in that trust.*

You know, your wisdom makes it really hard to have teenage angst.

It is why dragons are partnered with young mortals. We even you out.

It was good talking to you, Chine. I'll see you in a bit.

You as well, Dustling.

Alex spent the rest of her walk thinking through what he had said. There were a lot of things to take into consideration, but the dragon was right.

Myrddin and the Nest trusted her.

She needed to believe in that trust.

It was kind of funny. There'd been a moment earlier in the day when Alex had been worried about adjusting to not being special anymore. Then, the moment she started talking to the dragon, all she could talk about was the stress of that weight.

Things seemed to make a little more sense now, even if they weren't clear, just a cloudy, amorphous blob of emotions. They weren't bad emotions, and deep down, Alex knew what she had to do: the weapon had to be destroyed. There would be other ways to get rid of the Dark One. Alex didn't know what they were going to be, but she was certain they'd figure them out.

The base was no more than a block ahead. Most of the houses were empty. Alex figured that was the only way a top-secret military base could have been plopped down in the middle of her town without anyone noticing it. The whole town was probably a shell. Talk about a coincidence.

Or was it?

Alex had never thought about how Myrddin had known to watch her through VR. She'd been playing for years. Just how long had she been a subject of interest to Myrddin and the Nest?

As Alex let these thoughts play out in her head, she started walking near a convoy of military SUVs. *There's no way all this could have been built just to watch me.*

She heard a loud click like the sound of a door being unlocked very loudly. It came from the convoy. She looked in the direction of the sound, seeing an SUV's rear hatch open.

A glowing white orb fell out the back of the SUV. *What the hell is that?* Alex thought.

Then the orb brightened and there was a loud screech as it exploded outward.

The last thing Alex saw was the brightness of the light as she felt her body rising into the air.

Then all was black.

CHAPTER SIX

Alex woke up in the med-bay of the military base, nurses all around her. They were treating her wounds and Alex instinctively reached out to push them away. They fell to the floor

She looked down at her hands, caught off guard by what she had done. Alex had assumed that the telekinesis she'd experienced in Vardis' dream was limited to dreams.

Obviously, that assumption was wrong.

The nurses got back on their feet, undeterred by Alex pushing them away. They got back to work, wielding Nest healing devices.

Alex's body was covered in minor cuts and bruises, and the nurses were working hard at treating them. The wounds on her chest and shoulder from the dream had already been attended to.

Once the nurses stopped bustling about, Alex was able to ask one of them what happened. The nurse explained that the base had been under attack. Multiple bombs on their convoy of supplies had detonated. It was assumed by the upper brass that there was a double agent somewhere in the base who had given away the delivery time.

Alex bit her tongue and didn't say anything about Vardis.

If she was going to talk to someone about this, it was going to be much higher up the chain. Vardis could be dangerous. If that attack had come from him, there was no telling how many people he was willing to put at risk for his goals.

But Alex already knew how many people Vardis would risk: an entire universe. What were a few measly human soldiers in the grand scheme of his plans?

As the nurses prepared to leave, one of them leaned over Alex and whispered in her ear, "We took care of your other wounds too. They should heal pretty well. Be safe out there."

Alex didn't know what to say, so she merely nodded and smiled, muttering a quiet thank you. Once the nurses were gone, she sat up, preparing to get out of bed.

A loud beep came from her dragon anchor. She looked down at it and saw there was an incoming call from Abby. Alex picked up and said, "Hello?"

Abby's face shone brightly on the anchor. "Hey! How's it — Oh, crap, what happened to you?"

Alex brought the anchor closer to her face so that Abby couldn't see the extent of the wounds. "Oh, you know, just the usual explosion. Nothing too bad. I should be back on my feet in no time."

"Well, I'm glad you're sitting down because I wanted to talk to you about the readings I got from the shard. It looks like there might be some kind of living creature—"

Alex sighed as she shook her head. "A living creature residing within the shard with an unbelievable amount of energy?"

Abby gave Alex a confused look. "Hey, if you don't need me running experiments on—"

"No, it's not that. Well, you wouldn't believe me if I told you."

"Try me."

Alex tried to sum up everything she experienced the night before into a clear, concise statement. That wasn't happening. "Okay, so I got pulled into the dream of an interdimensional being and walked through all of his memories, and I saw he's planning on destroying our reality to take out the Dark One with some kind of ancient being that used to plague their planet or something. And now I have telekinesis, and I don't know how, but my telepathy is also much stronger." Alex took a deep breath. "Everything is terrible, and I'm not sure what I'm supposed to do, and yeah, it's all the worst."

Abby stared at Alex through the anchor screen, her eyes narrow as if she were trying to process everything Alex had said. "Wait, you have telepathy?"

"You're missing the point!"

"No, I got everything else. Still working through it. Anybody else know about this alien? Or just you?"

Alex shook her head as she shrugged, sending two different meanings. "Well, I mean, Myrddin has his suspicions. And Boundless is pretty much on the same page."

"So, what's the big problem? Have Myrddin pull the plug."

"It's not that simple. Myrddin still isn't sure. And I'm only sure as far as I trust dreams, and not even my dream, someone else's. I can think of a ton of better places to start for proving someone else guilty of wanting to cause interdimensional genocide."

"Point taken. On another note, how's the arm holding up?"

Alex looked down at her bionic arm, stretching her fingers out and then making a fist. "Good as the day I got it. Why are you asking?"

Abby pulled up a chart that projected on Alex's anchor. "You've been showing a spike in your body processing draconic fluid. I wanted to make sure you weren't burning hot or anything. All right, I've got to go. You just dropped a lot on me. Gonna try to get that intel to someone who can do something 'bout it. Stay frosty, snow-girl."

"Snow-girl?"

"Shut up, I'm not in the DGA because I'm witty. Bye."

Abby hung up, leaving Alex to her thoughts, which were instantly interrupted by a sarcastic voice saying, "Are you approved for inter-faculty discussions?"

Roy stood in the doorway, gnawing on his cigar. His swagger was a little more tame than usual, no doubt to show that he took Alex's injuries seriously.

She groaned loudly as she laid back. "Are you kidding me? Am I not allowed to talk to people?"

"Only when it seems like you're talking about sensitive information. Which I have no doubt you are doing right now."

Alex leaned over to see if there was anyone behind Roy. "Come in and close the door."

"You're joking, right?"

"No."

Roy stepped into the room and closed the door behind himself. "What do you have for me? Because you're obviously sharing it with everyone else."

"It's not like that. *She* called *me*. Abby said she was going to be passing it along to you and Myrddin anyway, but I want you to hear it from me first. I've already talked to Boundless about my suspicions about Vardis."

Roy pulled a seat up to Abby's bed as he chuckled. "Yeah, you and everyone else. What dirt do you have on the guy?"

Abby couldn't believe what she'd just heard. "Wait, you

make it sound like there are tons of people who don't trust him."

"Do you think we're stupid? We run an interspecies military program that spans nine realms. Of course, no one trusts a guy who just shows up one day and says he has a weapon to kill the Dark One. You have any idea how many insurance scammers Myrddin has had me wade through?"

Alex laughed so hard she had to grab her ribs. "Wait, you're putting this guy on par with an insurance scam?"

"A scam is a scam. Now, what do you have for me?"

For the second time in ten minutes, Alex had to try to find a way to explain what had happened the night before. Thankfully, she'd practiced with Abby. "Last night, Vardis drew me into one of his dreams via that telepathic link I told Myrddin about. I saw what he was planning to do with the weapon. What it can actually do."

Roy put his cigar away. "I'm assuming it doesn't involve needing my social security."

"No."

"Good, because I don't have any. Neither do you, by the way. Myrddin wipes us clean when we sign on, but after this is over, you're going to have *really* good credit."

Alex couldn't believe Roy was being so flippant. "Are you messing with me, or do you really not care about any of this?"

Roy threw his hands up defensively. "No, no, not at all. I'm not bothered by you telling me that you got information on Vardis from a psychic dream. Honestly, it's not the weirdest thing I've heard today. It *might* be the most normal thing."

Alex was surprised. She hadn't been expecting to hear that, and it was probably the best news she'd gotten all day. "Wait, you believe me?"

"Of course, I believe you. Myrddin already knows you

have a weird-ass link with Vardis. Did you think he hadn't mentioned it to me? One of the first things you learn in PsyOps is that dream-to-dream contact is a valuable form of espionage."

Alex nearly leaped up at Roy's words. She hadn't been expecting to be believed so readily. "So, we can go get him and put a stop to this whole—"

"Hold on. Before you get your hopes up, dreams are the same as most other espionage, which means it needs to be validated. I can't make decisions based on anything that doesn't have three or more sources."

Alex stared at Roy, almost unable to comprehend what he was saying. "You're telling me we have to sit here and wait until Vardis shows us that he's trying to destroy the whole universe?"

Roy stood up and ruffled Alex's hair, which made her want to grab his arm and snap it off. "No, I'm not saying that. What I'm saying is that we've got a plan in motion in case Vardis tries anything. Trust me, we're not going to let him have free rein on this one."

"Okay, so when do we go?"

Roy looked down at Alex, glancing at her wounds. "You aren't going anywhere for the time being. Nurses said that you have pretty extensive injuries. Two of those are much more serious than the rest and were patched up before the accident."

Alex didn't think she was going to get Roy to budge on the topic and decided to try another tack. "What was that explosion? The one that took me out?"

Roy's face became serious as he nervously scratched his beard. "We've been trying to figure that one out. All we could find was shrapnel, and we're trying to—

"It came from Vardis. He was responsible."

Roy laughed uneasily and said, "Okay, I know he is under

suspicion, but that doesn't mean we have to blame him for every single thing that—"

"Trust me, Roy. It was him. He knows what I saw last night, and he wants to keep me from stopping him. What better way than putting me in the hospital so that I can drown in bureaucracy?"

"What? You never even have to *touch* the paperwork."

Alex started to get out of bed. Her chest and shoulders still hurt, but they were manageable. "I can't believe I'm arguing about this with you. You're not putting me on the sidelines. If Vardis is out there, I'm going to be as well."

Roy tried to shoo Alex back to her bed. "Hey, hey, hold on. You still need bed rest. You've been going nonstop since the last mission, and even *I'm* starting to think you might need time to recuperate."

"Are you saying I can't do my job?"

Roy shook his head as he backed away. "No, I'm saying you're very high-strung at the moment. This is something we can take care of, so maybe stop trying to hold the world on your shoulders."

"I'm not stressed out, Roy! There's—"

Alex was cut off by a siren blaring through the military base. "What's that?"

Roy pulled up his HUD and scrolled through a few messages. "Shit! The base is under attack."

"By what?"

Roy looked up for a moment, his eyes searching for an answer. "They don't know yet. But it looks—"

The lights in the room started to flicker. Alex went to grab her shirt, and her hand stopped moving. She struggled, but nothing happened. Then she was thrown against the wall as if someone had picked her up and tossed her.

Roy stopped in his tracks and stared at her. "What the hell is going on?"

The light fixture from the ceiling ripped off and flew toward Alex, who was barely able to get out of the way in time.

Glass skittered all over the floor as Roy and Alex backed away from the fixture. "Vardis," Alex growled.

CHAPTER SEVEN

The lights went out, and Alex and Roy stood in the darkness.

Another light fixture came flying at Alex, and she jumped to the right, dodging it. "We need to get out of here," she shouted.

Roy looked around the room as the lights tried to flicker back on. "What's going on?"

"I have no idea, but I know we can't stay here to find out."

Alex hit her dragon anchor, causing her rider armor to pour over her skin. That was better. Now she felt like she was ready to get down to business. She opened and closed her bionic fist as she headed for the door, then whipped it open and stepped forward, Roy close behind her.

They two of them stepped into a lab, the one Alex had seen in Vardis' dream. The only difference was, this time the lab had five Vardises.

Not aliens of the same species, five Vardises.

Roy drew his pistol and aimed at one of the aliens. "Okay, no. We need to stop now, and you need to tell me what the hell is going—"

Before Roy could finish his sentence, his feet lifted off the ground. His eyes went wide as he flew across the room, hit the wall hard, and crumpled to the floor.

Alex didn't hesitate. She drew her scythe, aware that the energy was coming from her and not from the dragon anchor. She dove forward, slashing at one of the Vardises, who faded into a white mist when it was hit. She went on the next, managing to catch it with an uppercut before she was gripped by a psychic hand and tossed at Roy.

She smashed into the wall and fell on her back, rolled over, and shook Roy back into consciousness. It was surprising that hitting a wall was enough to knock Roy out. Alex had seen him walk away from injuries that made the psychic attack look like a mosquito bite.

That was what this was. Alex had put it together. Vardis *did* know that she'd been in his dream. The attack on her way to the military base had only been the first step, the physical aspect. Now the alien was coming for her mind.

He must have drawn them into a psychic realm, or maybe he was projecting his own. Alex had no idea. She'd never been much into comic books. If Jim were here, he probably could have explained the whole thing.

The three remaining versions of Vardis were floating toward Alex, their eyes glowing a piercing white, energy crackling from them.

Alex helped Roy to his feet, the older man looking as if he were ready to pass out again. "You have to get it together, Roy! I need you in this fight. Last time, I hardly got out of here."

Roy looked at Alex, his face green like he was ready to vomit. Then he straightened up and aimed his pistol. "I'm assuming we're in trouble or something wants to kill us."

Alex pointed at the approaching aliens. "Vardis. He wants to kill us."

Roy leaned over and threw up.

Great, Alex thought.

The three versions of Vardis laughed as they watched Roy retching. "I didn't think the humans would be so easy to kill," one of them said.

Another turned to his doppelganger and smiled. "No, neither did—"

A shot rang out and echoed in the lab. Roy fired two more times, not bothering to straighten up while still wiping the bile from his mouth.

Two of the aliens stumbled backward, holding their chests. One sneered. "Foolish human. This is not the physical realm. You—"

Roy coughed loudly and held up his hand, silencing the alien as he straightened up. "Hold on, hold on. Psychic realm and yeah, bullets don't work, got to—"

He fired three more shots and each hit an alien in the chest, tearing open a hole nearly the size of Alex's head. They fell to their knees before bursting into white light.

Roy leaned against the wall, trying to catch his breath as Alex ran over to him. "How did you do that?" she asked. "That was amazing! I didn't know you were a psychic."

The mech rider shook his head as he straightened up, looking as if he were finally acclimating to his new environment. "Not a psychic, but I've been doing drills with Myrddin for years. You know, in case someone tries to invade my mind or pull shit like this. Sorry, language, it'll take a couple of minutes for me to be on top of my game, but I'll be able to hold my own. Especially if all he's going to be throwing at us are projections."

Alex was annoyed that Roy had a better handle on things than she did, even while he was sick to his stomach. She was also happy to have someone around who knew what the hell was going on. "What do you mean, projections?"

Roy stumbled away from the wall and toward the piles of white ash on the ground, pointing at one with his pistol. "Those aren't Vardis. This whole place—whatever we're seeing, the whole plane—that's Vardis. The most he'll be able to do if he's planning on keeping us here is send out projections of his subconscious. They're only a fraction of his strength."

"How much do you know about this stuff?"

Roy tried to hide his smug smile. "I've been fighting the Dark One for a lot longer than it looks like, and I've run across my fair share of psychics in the past. As they say, this isn't my first rodeo. And since we already took care of the projections here, Vardis will probably change things up. Give us a new place to fight and hope we'll be thrown off by it."

Alex thought back to Vardis' dream. That was why the realm had kept jumping locations and time. It had been his mind attempting to get the advantage by confusing Alex with different scenarios. "So, what are we supposed to do?"

Roy was walking around the room as if he didn't have a care in the world. The disorientation of being in a psychic plane had apparently worn off. "I don't know, look around? Unless you've been here before."

Alex walked over to the table in the middle of the lab and called Roy over. "In a dream. His dream. This was where I found out about the weapon." She picked up the scroll and tossed it to Roy.

Roy skimmed through the notes. "Hm, looks like Vardis was a bigshot scientist on his world, and old as hell. This whole project, using the shard for creating kin, was his idea."

"Wait, you can read that?"

"Yeah, can't you?"

Roy handed the scroll back to Alex. She took a look and realized she could read the alien writing as easily as if it were braille. "When I was in his dream, I couldn't read any of this. I studied it for a while too. What changed?"

Roy was wandering around the room again. "He's probably got more defenses up while he's dreaming—basic PsyOps training—but his attention is split right now. There's only so much you can concentrate on at a time."

The walls of the lab started to shake, then broke apart, allowing light to shine through the cracks. "Looks like we're moving," Roy muttered under his breath.

Air shifted from cold and sterile to hot and fetid. Alex struggled to breathe. She felt like she was going to suffocate.

Roy seemed to be in the same situation. His eyes were wild as he looked around, the walls tearing themselves down and the ground roiling.

The room shattered into multiple versions of itself, some small, others larger, like a fun-house mirror. They slammed into each other as Alex and Roy floated through the darkness, which abruptly stopped, then congealed into a new reality.

Alex and Roy stood in what looked like a jungle. It wasn't similar to anything Alex had seen in her books at the Nest, though. This wasn't Earth.

Before the two of them was a group of human soldiers. They weren't wearing Army fatigues. The colors were reminiscent of an elvish sigil Alex had seen at the Nest. "Where are we?"

Roy was muttering under his breath, backing away from the small group of humans. "No," he muttered.

Alex turned away from the crowd of soldiers to Roy. "Where are we?"

"One of the moons in the elvish cluster. Dorian."

"What are we doing here?"

Roy's eyes grew hard and cold as he swallowed and pulled out his cigar. He lit it, and his composure came back. "Vardis is playing mind games. Guess he has access to our memories as well as his. He's stronger than I thought."

"This is your memory?"

Roy pointed at the crowd of soldiers with his cigar. "Oh, yeah, this is mine. That's me over there." He headed for the soldiers, motioning for Alex to follow him.

The soldiers were crouched around a dead body covered in a white shroud. Alex didn't recognize Roy's face in any of the soldiers, not even a younger Roy. "Which one are you?" she asked.

Roy nodded at the body under the shroud. "Right there. Go ahead. They shouldn't notice you if you do anything."

Alex wasn't certain she could, but her hand was moving before she realized it, forced by curiosity. She pulled the shroud back.

A younger Roy stared up at Alex, the side of his face blown off, his jaw hanging loose from his cheekbone. His skull was fractured, blood pooling into his dirty hair. "Oh, my God!" Alex leaned over and threw up, unable to keep her horror in her stomach.

Roy knelt next to his dead body. He held the head up and looked into his own eyes. "Yeah, this one wasn't fun." He pulled out his pistol, and before Alex could say anything, shot the soldiers, causing them to burst into white smoke.

Alex screamed and backed away from Roy. "What are you doing? Are you crazy?"

Roy shook his head as he pressed the gun to the younger version of his head. "No, I'm not. He's trying to mess with my head. Apparently, he thought this would be enough to rattle me. He doesn't know *I* know what's going on, or he hasn't gone through my memories enough to know this isn't the first time I've seen my dead body. Ain't gonna rattle me."

Roy pulled the trigger.

The jungle started to pull apart at the edges as if an earthquake were shaking everything loose.

Alex stared at Roy, looking from his dead face to his living one, which was much more disturbed than he was letting on. "What happened?"

Roy holstered his gun and stood up, watching the jungle around him shrivel, the leaves of the trees falling down en masse, the roots tearing up the earth. "It's not important, and it's not a conversation to have sober. That means you still have another six years before you're going to hear about it unless you get lucky and Vardis finds a useful memory."

Roy turned his attention to Alex, his eyes as focused and as determined as when he had pulled the trigger on himself. "He's going to come after you too. That's why this is all taking so long. He's looking for ways to break us. Crack the mind and the body follows—oldest rule in the book. Wherever he takes us, remember that it's not real. Whatever he shows you, it's a lie, even if you think it's happened before. He'll distort it, and you won't even realize it. Don't trust anything but me."

Alex swallowed as she thought of the prospects. "You trust me too, right?"

Roy smiled, and it was a sad sight. "Of course, I trust you. Now get ready."

CHAPTER EIGHT

Alex and Roy woke up in a car.

They were in the backseat, buckled up next to each other. There was a child sitting between them, strapped into a car seat.

There were two people in the front seats, but Alex couldn't see who they were. She had a strong feeling she knew the people in the front seats and she'd been in this car before, but she couldn't remember when.

Then the woman driving the car looked back as she made cooing sounds to the child in the car seat. It was Claire, Alex's mom.

Alex tried to catch her mother's attention, but Claire was only focused on the baby. "Mom?" she asked quietly.

Roy seemed to still be getting his bearings. He looked much less comfortable than when he was in his own memories but not nearly as bad as when the psychic attack had first started.

Alex, on the other hand, was extremely disoriented at being in a scene she couldn't remember. This had happened long ago, and she'd been only a child. It was like watching a surreal television show starring her parents. Further, the child in the car seat was not blind. She could see it in the way the child tracked her mother's movements.

George, who was sitting next to Claire, rapped on the dashboard with his knuckles and said, "Don't forget, we have to go to the grocery store before we head home."

Claire turned back to the road, and the emotional climate in the car chilled. "You don't have to remind me of every errand we have to run as soon as we get out of the house," she barked.

Alex jumped at the sound of her mother's voice. She'd never heard Claire take that tone. It obviously frightened the child in the car seat as well. The child had tensed up when Claire spoke.

The car was quiet for a second, then George exploded. The air in the car turned red. Alex couldn't understand most of the words her father was saying, but she felt them deep in her chest, a sickening gripping around the inside of her throat, falling with the weight of a thousand hammers.

It was getting hotter. Alex could feel sweat beading on her forehead. She wanted to leave, to get out of the car, to be anywhere but where she was at the moment. She tried to open the door, but it was child-locked from the inside.

The child was uncomfortable as well. Alex could now see it wasn't a baby. The kid was at least five, maybe even seven.

Roy had the window down as far as it would go and was trying to catch his breath. "It's not real, Alex."

In the front of the car, Claire faced George, her face contorting as fire leaped from her eyes. What came out of her mouth was as hot as dragon fire and ten times louder than George's tirade had been.

The words hung in the air as if they were blades repurposed for the guillotine. Some of the words did not remain stationary, though. They flew between Claire and George, slicing their faces.

Blood streamed down her parents' faces. It was pooling on their seats.

Some of the blades flew into the back. Alex covered her head, trying to shield herself as the child cried and cried, blades occasionally nicking them. "Cover your damn face!" Alex shouted at the child.

She covered her mouth. She had no idea why she had shouted at the kid. None of this was the kid's fault. None of it. But she still contributed to the heat in the car, the stifling heat that was making her head swim.

Roy had the right idea. Alex cracked her window and stuck her head out, breathing in the fresh, cool air. Outside, it was night. The stars shone above, and a cool breeze ran through the neighborhood.

Something tugged her shirt. When she looked inside, it was the crying child. Remaining in the car was the last thing Alex wanted to do. There was the screaming of her parents and the wailing of the child, plus Roy's pathetic whimpering. The car was hell.

But the kid shouldn't be crying. Alex knew that. On a deep level, she knew it was wrong that the child was upset, and if the adults in the front of the car wouldn't deal with it, Alex would.

Alex rolled her window down farther but sat back. She grabbed the child's hand and tried to comfort her, but nothing came out of her mouth, just a stifled groan.

At that noise, Claire and George turned and screamed at the child, shrill screeches that tore through Alex's eardrums. She and the child covered their ears, trying to block the sound.

"Why don't you just shut up?"

Claire and George were silent now, their jaws hanging

open, nearly touching their chests. Their eyes were hollow, and the muscles of their faces were as slack as loose rope.

Alex didn't know who had given the command, but she was glad someone had because it was finally silent.

There were two bright lights outside the window on the left. Alex only halfway noticed since she was so relieved the noise had stopped, but then metal crunched and the world went topsy-turvy. She noticed glass hanging above her head as the car tumbled through the air.

It hit the ground once and continued to roll, finally stopping on its side and spinning.

Alex coughed up blood as she tried to unbuckle her seatbelt. Roy was also trying to get out of his restraints. He had a gash across his forehead and was coughing up blood.

The blood from the front seat was now pooling in the back. Alex saw it dripping down the walls of the car. She had to get out or she was going to drown, but she was trapped. She was going to die in this car, choking on the blood of her parents.

"It's not real," Roy muttered. "You're not a child. You're a dragonrider."

At those words, Alex let out a mighty telekinetic blast that tore the door off the car, then reached down to help Roy get out. She'd noticed the child wasn't in the car anymore. "Where is she?" Alex shouted.

Roy grabbed Alex by the shoulder and tried to pull her away from the wreck. "We need to get out of here. You don't need to see this."

Alex pushed Roy's hand away and followed a trail of glass and blood to wailing.

The child was cradled in Claire's and George's arms, its face covered in glass, blood pouring from its eyes as it thrashed and cried.

George was trying to calm the child, whispering, "It's

okay, Alex. It's going to be okay," as Claire stood and started pacing, chewing on her fingernails.

Alex touched the sides of her face, the scars in her skin that her parents had always told her were from a cat scratch. "I wasn't born blind?"

Roy stormed over to Alex and stood between her and the vision of her parents. "It's not real! Vardis is messing with your head!"

A psychic blast ripped out from Alex, sending Roy back a few steps. "What do you mean, it's not real! Your vision happened! You said so yourself. Just because this isn't real, it doesn't mean this didn't happen!"

Alex turned back to her parents, rage seething out of her in flashes of telekinesis. *They're the reason I spent my entire life in the dark. Because of their selfish fighting.*

Claire looked up at Alex's approach, but there was something off in her face. It didn't quite look human. The forehead was huge, bulging out, and her body was unusually muscled. It was enough to stop Alex in her tracks. "Mom?" she asked.

Claire stretched out her arms toward Alex as if begging for a hug, then her jaw fell open as her head lolled back, a sound coming from her mouth like that of a mewling cat and a dying goat. The inhuman sound conveyed no meaning, only dread.

When Alex looked at George and the younger version of herself, she saw the same thing. George and the child were whining too, the combined sounds like a war siren going off.

The child flopped onto the concrete, lifting herself up by her arms, blood pooling under her eyes as she shook violently. "They hated you, Alex! That's why they fought. They never wanted you. You took everything from them. They were happy before you."

Two bones shot out of the child's feet, bending backward

as the child pushed herself up with her chubby arms. She was foaming at the mouth and making uneven motions toward Alex like a cat that had had stilts forced onto its paws. "When you came, they lost everything, and then you went and lost your eyes. Do you know what their lives were like, caring for their pathetic, blind freak of a daughter?"

Alex lashed the creature with a psychic blast, but it did nothing. "You're a liar!"

The child's head tilted to the side as her face melted down to the skull. Vardis' skull. "Me? Lie? Never!"

The baby Vardis stood on its bony legs as flesh and blood oozed over them, the chubby arms of the child stretching as Vardis' head burst out of the child's shoulder. The creature leaned on its front arms in the fashion of a gorilla, pus and blood oozing from the wounds in its face.

A telekinetic blast hit Alex and she slammed into the wreckage of the car, stumbling to her feet as another one came at her. She barely threw a weak shield up in time to protect her before she fell again. "They don't love me."

Roy ran over to Alex and scooped her up in his arms before taking cover behind the car. He darted out and took three shots at the creature shuffling toward them.

The bullets ripped through the baby creature, but it only paused for a moment, then continued its slow, jerky movements.

Roy shook Alex hard. "You need to get it together. I can't do as much damage in your head as I can in mine, even less when you're in this state. He's messing with your mind. This isn't real. It's not true, not in the way he's showing it."

Alex shook her head as she fought back tears. "I don't know what's true. I don't know."

"Alex, if you don't sort this out, Vardis is going to win. I need you."

Alex covered her face with her hands. She couldn't hear

Roy. She couldn't hear anything. She couldn't see anything. "Oh, my God, I can't see! Roy, I can't see."

Roy popped out and fired again. "What do you mean, you can't see?"

Tears rolled down Alex's face as she held her hand out in front of her. She was back in the blackness, or maybe she'd never left. "I'm blind."

Then the ground fell out from under them as the air filled with the wailing of the creature in the darkness.

CHAPTER NINE

Time is meaningless without context. A minute does not matter without the seconds preceding it. There is an environment in which time must exist. Darkness is not that environment, nor is silence.

It was here that Alex found herself. She wasn't aware of how long she'd been here or how long it had taken her to go gibbering into madness, but somewhere long ago, she had forgotten who she was. She sat in the darkness, ruminating on her life. At times she stood and tried to find her way back, but she did not know what to return to.

The descent was gradual. If she had been aware, she would have tried to hold onto sanity longer, but unfortunately, she clung to the wrong thing.

The last thing Alex saw was her parents screaming as the chubby abomination Vardis had created limped toward her.

Alex could see now that it had been a trap, but she couldn't figure out how to escape it. The more she thought, the more disgusted she was with her parents. With their voices in the car. With the way they had stood mute and dumb around her, too covered in their own shit to have the wherewithal to have called an ambulance.

She probably wouldn't have lost her sight if they had.

She descended into the darkness. Reaching a depth she had never seen before.

At the bottom of this darkness was a fire that cast no light. Alex only knew it was there because of the heat. She found it one night, and she huddled next to it, shivering since the fire was not enough to fight the cold wind that cut through her body like the blades her parents had shouted at each other.

Near the fire, Alex screamed. She screamed for someone to save her, but she could not remember any names. By the time she thought to call for help, she hardly remembered her own.

Near primordial in her existence, she hunched over the flames and forgot how to speak, only able to remember language as a rudimentary instrument that did not give her the tools necessary to convey what existed within her.

Yet even in the darkness, something began to change. She did not need words for it, nor did she need her eyes.

As the flames flickered, she whispered to herself, guttural sounds that could have come from an animal. She knew they were not the sounds of a human, much like she knew the mud and gunk that clung to her skin wasn't hers. Nor was this an extended period of time without food. If it was, a person would have died.

This deduction brought forth the next.

People didn't live forever, but she could not be dead. Her last memory was watching herself with serious but not deadly injuries. But there was more: vague outlines that shimmered like constellations in the night sky. Then there came the first inkling of light. Hardly noticeable, pulsing as if it had a heartbeat.

Alex turned from the black flames, resting her back against them, staring up at these skeletons of memories. She thought long and deep in the place with no words and over-laid muscle and flesh on the bones floating above her.

She had lived in the darkness most of her life. There she had built worlds and carved her memories of what she'd heard into neat, precise instruments. She listened to each one.

As she recalled to her mother's voice on her fifth birthday as her father helped her cut a cake, she trickled the images of her mother and father that she had from after she received her eye implants. She imagined what they would look like, talking to each other.

Then she forced herself to remember the crash. Compared the faces. One set looked weaker than the other, the faces shifting and changing, the voices contorting.

Above, the sky brightened.

For the first time in what felt like decades, Alex looked down at her hands. Her fingers were thick and knobby, dirt under her nails.

Whatever this place was, Alex realized she was not a prisoner, or not in the sense that someone could keep her here. She'd been keeping herself here.

"Where are you?"

Alex turned to the flames warming her body. Then, for reasons she could not understand, she flung her arm into the fire.

The pain was immediate and then vanished. Alex looked down at her hand. It wasn't made of flesh. It was bionic.

If you're ever in a dream, pinch yourself to wake up.

Someone had told her that at some time. A long time ago.

"Roy, where are you?"

Alex stood and walked away from the flames, following the faint light cast by the fleshed-out constellations above. As she wandered away from the fire, the world around her got brighter.

The feeling inside Alex, nameless and hateful, grew stronger, but it was not directed at her parents. That had been a lie. She couldn't prove it, but she knew it was. No, this feeling was directed at whoever had told her the lie.

Vardis had planted a seed, and it had taken root for too long. Alex didn't know how much time she'd lost, but she was going to find him and make him pay.

There was another reason Alex needed to find Vardis. She wasn't sure about it, but it was more important than cramming his stupid face up his ass, and it was far beyond her as a person. She'd find it when she did.

"Roy, where the hell *are* you!"

Alex reached into what was left of the darkness and tore it apart, ripping it as if it were a silk veil. Then there was light.

She could see Roy.

The man was old, older than Alex had assumed he was. His hair and beard were gray, and he had a cane. He was leaning against a pile of red mud.

As Alex stepped into the light, she started to be able to make sense of the world around her.

The world she looked upon was Vardis' home, but it was different than the vision of his world in his dream.

There were mountains of red mud. Lakes of it, as far as the eye could see. An entire world of clay.

Alex ran over to Roy and helped him sit up. His eyes were gray and glaucous. He murmured under his breath as Alex tried to get him to his feet, "Who are you?"

"It's me, Alex."

"I can't see anything. I can't see anything. I think I'm dying. Finally. This time it's the real thing."

Alex looked around. She had no idea what to do. Digging

herself out of wherever the hell she had been was one thing. Getting Roy out was another problem altogether. "It isn't real, Roy. None of this is real. That's what you told me. It's all in our heads. Or in Vardis'. But it isn't real."

Roy slumped to the side, knocking his cane over. "What is real? These aren't my memories. I've never been blind. Been this old but never been this blind before."

"Are you going to get up or just sit here moping?"

Roy rested his head on the clay behind him and chuckled. "You're one to talk. I'm pretty sure you've been in the shit as long as I have. How the hell did you get out?"

Alex looked down at her bionic arm. "You pinch yourself when you're dreaming."

"What?"

Alex drew Roy's gun from its holster, then took his hand and wrapped his fingers around the butt. "You pinch yourself when you're dreaming."

Roy looked at Alex, his eyes milky. "When you're dreaming?"

Alex pressed the muzzle of the pistol to Roy's leg. "Yeah. When you're dreaming."

Roy pulled the trigger.

The pistol blasted a hole the size of an apple. He screamed in pain and cupped the wound with his hand, trying to keep the blood from flowing.

As Roy swore under his breath, the cloudiness in his eyes started to fade. He continued to swear, finally taking a deep breath and grabbing his cane. "Would have thought you went to PsyOps after pulling a stunt like that."

Roy tried to stand, and Alex gave him a hand. They both took some time to gaze upon the red world, its red suns hanging above them like a promise of hell. "So, this is what the bastard is capable of when he's awake."

"How bad was it for you?"

As Roy answered, his body got younger. "Pretty bad. Ain't proud to say it, but I was lost in there for a while. In myself. Or him. I don't know the difference. But he broke me. You?"

Alex watched the red suns above her. "Almost. But I wouldn't be here if he had, would I?"

Roy reached into his pocket and pulled out two cigars. He handed one to Alex. "Don't light it," he said. "That one's just herbs and crap, but it'll help ground you. Kinda like pinching yourself over and over."

Alex accepted the fake cigar and gnawed on it. The thing tasted like chocolate and rosemary. "Now what?"

"We break out of the attack. Vardis probably assumes we're done, but he's at a disadvantage. He's been keeping up two worlds, or maybe even three. He's stretched himself pretty thin. There's no way he'll know we've broken free. He's too busy concentrating on keeping everything running smoothly. Now we take the fight to him."

"How are we going to do that? We were hardly able to tell the difference between reality and this?"

Roy lit his cigar and shook his head. "Not true. We both knew it wasn't real, if only on a subconscious level. Or at least you did."

One of the clay mountains exploded into fire. The smoke rose to the sky, obscuring something that had been lurking there. She pointed at it and Roy followed her finger, jumping in fear when he got a glimpse of what was behind the smoke. *"What the hell is that?"*

Millions of eyes peered out from behind the smoke as lightning crackled through the clouds. "That's what's in the shard," Alex explained. "They found a way to trap it thousands of years ago. This is what the kin are made out of—some kind of elder god."

Roy was looking at his pistol. "I swear, there's a new elder god every twenty years or so. This ain't anything special. Just means something is old enough to remember before there was anything. But we need to go on the offensive. The longer we stay docile, the faster he'll find us."

Alex turned away from the eyes that were peering at her. "Fine. We take this to Vardis. I haven't done PsyOps before. What do they tell you to do in situations like this?"

Roy kicked at the clay next to him. "They tell us to go deep. Deeper than the person attacking us would go, and I think we've already been that deep in ourselves. This could be what's deep for Vardis. This place. Let's take it deeper."

Alex thought it was a good idea. The alien had delved into her deeps. Why not give him the same experience? "Okay, but hold on. I want to see if we can get reinforcements."

She focused and brought her thoughts under control, strangling the wild ideas and concepts that were whirling in her head. After she had at least partially accomplished her goal, she reached out to Chine, but the most she was able to utter was a bestial cry for help.

What came back was something she had not experienced or expected: full and unadulterated rage from Chine. It was not directed at her, but at whoever had hurt her. *I am coming, Dustling. I am coming.*

Alex grabbed Roy and dragged him to a pool of mud that was a couple of yards away from them. "Chine is coming," she said. "I don't know when he's going to get here, but we aren't waiting. If we're going to bring the fight to Vardis, then we are."

The mud was shallow, hardly coming up to Alex's knees. "We find him now, no matter what."

Alex dropped to her knees and started digging into the mud, splashing it up as she crawled deeper and deeper into the wet red earth. She let out a psychic blast that carved into the ground as she pulled out her scythe, then she began cutting into the earth, ripping away mud and flinging it to the side as she continued to blast it.

Roy followed suit, dropping to his knees and digging with his hands, trying to get to whatever Alex was burrowing toward.

The two of them were going to get to Vardis no matter what.

CHAPTER TEN

The two dug into the earth, Alex feeling the wet clay on her hands. She was reminded of when she and her parents had spent hours in their garden, digging up weeds to tend plants her parents thought were worthwhile.

"Here we are."

Alex pulled back, uncertain of what she was retreating from.

Neither she nor Roy was in the red clay world anymore. This was a new place, blood and bone born from a life Alex could not understand.

The bones cried out for vengeance. They cried out for absolution.

For what, Alex could not know.

Roy was beside her, covered in the red gunk just as she was, trying to make sense of what they were experiencing. "This is his mind. Whatever he remembers."

Alex had not stopped excavating. "It doesn't matter. We're getting to the bottom of it."

Roy stepped back, watching Alex work. He pulled a cigar

from his pocket and started chomping on it, muttering under his breath before flinging himself to the mud once more and digging as best as he could. "We'll get to the bottom of this. We'll get to the bottom of it all."

Alex lost herself to the digging, to flinging mud and clay over her shoulders, tossing it aside, trying to find what was buried beneath all of the red earth.

Lo and behold, in the tiny bits of clay were creatures, small worms with faces. Their eyes seemed to peer into Alex's, asking questions that could not be answered or even given words. They leered, and Alex managed to return their gazes.

Worms forced themselves out of the ground. Massive things, their bodies nearly the size of a human's, pushed themselves out of the clay, writhing, their invisible mouths grasping for what could not be seen.

Up above, the heavens were covered in red clouds, lightning flashing, the red bleeding into the sky. Eyes opened all around her, watching, scheming, and understanding. "Don't look at the eyes," Alex shouted. "You can't look at the eyes."

Both of them, as if she had understood her own warnings, looked away from the sky of many winking eyes. They ignored it and dug deeper, their hands and nails filled with what could not be ignored.

Then there was thunder, a voice calling out. It was reminiscent of ancient days and voices that had come before words existed, a time when all that could be communicated was the raw feeling of existence.

Roy pulled back from it, trying to hide as well as he could.

Alex did not try to hide. She did not try to fight, merely accepted that there was hardly any control in this place, only what she took.

Chine! Chine, where are you?

In the millions of twinkling eyes above, Alex watched Vardis' face take shape. He looked down upon the two humans, smirking as his voice thundered throughout the psychic plane. It reminded Alex of when she had been in the comet, listening to the voice of the Dark One.

They were one and the same, Vardis and the Dark One.

Alex focused on reaching out to her dragon. *Please, you have to hear me. Please. I need you.*

The sky ripped itself apart, lightning streaking and thunder booming.

And then there was silence. No answer came. Chine's voice could not be heard.

Alex understood.

Chine was not coming. He couldn't hear her, and as long as she thought she needed him to save her from what she was experiencing, that was going to be her existence. She would always need someone to save her.

But she hadn't needed Roy. She hadn't needed the rest of Boundless. She hadn't needed Chine. None of them could help her make sense of what existed in her mind, and as long as she kept calling for them, she was never going to get anywhere.

Alex focused her intention on her hand. She felt energy welling around it, her knuckles swelling with power. Then she leaped into the air and drove her hand into the red earth as she landed, shattering it.

The world around her broke apart, the pieces trying to cling to each other but unable to hold on as the power of Alex's psychic blast reverberated throughout the dreamscape.

Alex let loose a scream of rage and pain, her body bursting into flame as she plowed through the earth, the draconic fluid in her igniting, surging through her, and bolstering her powers, sending her telepathic reach farther than she could ever have imagined.

The world around her started to dissolve, Vardis' screams echoing.

Suddenly, her dragon's head burst through the dream, looking as if he had just come tumbling through a wall. *Alex, Child of Dust!*

Alex ran up to him and threw her arms around his neck. *I'm here. Oh, thank God, you're here!*

Chine unleashed a torrent of ether fire.

Alex felt it burning in her as well, the flames on her body changing from yellow to black, mimicking the ones coming from her dragon.

Alex and Roy drew as close to Chine as they could while he burned everything near him.

The earth Alex had been burrowing into collapsed and the three of them dropped into a cavern.

Chine blew out a small burst of flame, enough to illuminate the cave. There was hardly anything in it, only darkness.

As the ground continued to break apart, Alex and Roy fell into a chasm with Chine. The dragon let loose a torrent of ether flames, and Alex's body was covered in the same.

Telekinetic blasts radiated from the dragonrider as the three dropped into the clay world of Vardis' ancestors.

Alex hit the ground hard, then struggled to her feet, clutching the aching wounds she had received in the last battle with Vardis. "Where are you? Show yourself!"

The earth shook, the walls trembling and quivering as something like a face forced its way through the red clay. It was Vardis, his jeweled forehead quivering as his beady black eyes peered at Alex. "Show myself? Perhaps you should show yourself."

A telepathic blast hit Alex, trying to bring up all of Vardis' renditions of her past, but she knew better now. She knew that none of this was real.

Alex wiped away Vardis' onslaught with a simple gesture. "I'm done with you," she shouted. "All of this. I'm done with all of it."

Vardis' head trembled, his skin boiling as he screamed in rage. "The Dark One must be defeated!"

Alex screamed back as Chine flew up behind her, blasting ether flames to consume the visage of Vardis before them.

Vardis squealed as his skin melted, as did the clay surrounding his body, pooling in a red lake that looked like blood. The alien's face bubbled up to the top of it.

Alex and Chine walked down to the small lake, Roy right behind them. The three looked at the miserable, melting face of Vardis. "End it, Chine," Alex ordered.

Chine scorched the lake and everything around it.

Alex and Roy were caught up in the flames and consumed by them.

Alex snapped awake in her bed in the medbay. She looked around, trying to figure out what the hell had just happened. "Roy, are you here?"

Roy coughed and rolled over. He was lying on the floor, trying to grab his cigar. "Yeah, I'm here. I'm here."

Alex let out a sigh of relief. "I can't believe we got through that. Jesus Christ."

The lights in the room flickered on and off, then went out.

The walls shook, and the air got hotter.

Alex looked up.

Vardis stood in the doorway, his eyes burning with a dark

light as he stepped into the medbay. "This is just the beginning, Alex," he growled.

What is the power of Vardis' weapon and once unleashed, can it be stopped? Read the epic conclusion of the Dragon Rider series!

My Dungeon Master hates me... Seriously. I must be the most difficult player ever.

I'm playing a dual class Barbarian/Sorcerer – with a twist. The backstory for my character is this:

He was one of the great barbarians of the Mountain Goliaths. They raided a village doing their thing: Killing, stealing, pillaging... when a great sorcerer came onto the scene and with a wave of his hand, killed half the barbarian raiders.

My guy – who takes on the name of his last great deed ... another reason why my DM hates me – was spared for reasons the barbarian doesn't really understand. Then he was trained to become a sorcerer himself. But given his intelligence is a 10 and his Wisdom is an 11, he's a terrible sorcerer. He pretty much can cast Jump and Light ... and that's it.

Anywhooo ... he was released with the instructions that he must "Raise someone worthy to heights unimagined."

The Multi-Named Barbarian took this to heart and went

forth where he met the adventuring party that my character is a part of now.

On their first adventure, the party is clearing out a bunch of goblins from a cave. One goblin in particular – Gibbles – catches Multi-Named's attention. The barbarian/sorcerer sees potential in the creature.

He sees a KING!

So for the rest of that session, I spent Charisma roll after Charisma roll (including wasting all my inspirations and advantages) to befriend the goblin.

Now I'm out to 'civilize' him … a lofty task, indeed, because my character has anger issues. (After all, he's a barbarian at heart.)

Multi-Named protects Gibbles, buys him clothes, stands up for him when some wayward villager sneers at him …

Multi-Named will only go on an adventure if he feels it will further Gibbles' destiny. (My character has refused to do things set out by the DM, as well as committed to ridiculous fights in the name of the goblin.)

And this is my oath (or rather, Multi-Named's oath): By the time this adventure is over, Gibbles will be a king.

Or Multi-Named will die trying.

Sigh… like I said, my DM hates me.

Gibbles: Before … and (soon to be) after pics …

PS – Do you think I can convince Michael to play DnD with me?

AUTHOR NOTES MICHAEL ANDERLE
MAY 28, 2020.

So Ramy asked in his author notes the question of whether or not you, our fair reader, thought I might play Dungeons and Dragons with him.

The short answer is perhaps and maybe.

The longer answer is I would like to watch recordings of Ramy playing Dungeons and Dragons before I commit fully. It has been decades, I believe, since I have played the game. I am sure I would become the point of focus to find out just how bad could we can screw up Michael if he's playing a game of Dungeons & Dragons with us.

Not really too sure I care to do this. It's like being asked to be the one sitting on that little chair and getting dumped into a vat of ice-cold water. Everyone supports the fact that it's for charity. I'm pretty good with just putting up $200 and calling us square.

I've never been good at making a fool of myself. I can do that all on my lonesome without making a concerted effort to accomplish it. Sometimes, I wonder what would happen if I tried to be foolish. Probably I would fail, yet by not trying, I make it seem easy.

I can imagine that if I were being paid based on the amount of laughter, I might become a rich man indeed.

However, his question brings up questions of my own. I have watched a few YouTube series, and maybe a few television series, where the characters on the shows played Dungeons and Dragons. Yet, I don't know of any of them that have made me wish to watch the second show.

Is it that I'm just not a fan? Or is it that no one has successfully captured the joy and the freedom of playing a role-playing game? Is there perhaps an opportunity to create an online training course for actors on how to act while playing Dungeons and Dragons? Is there something that brings the joy that one feels when reading about Dungeons and Dragons events in someone's life?

I have read posts on the website Reddit from many people who have shared game experiences that have left me in stitches.

So, if someone can commit to text, why is it acting is so much more of a problem? Is it just that we bring our own experiences when we read it, but it is not capable of being captured on film?

Or is it that I have not seen these videos yet? I would love to!

Feel free, if you leave a review, to mention some of those in it. Or, drop by one of our Facebook groups and talk about it. In general, you can find me on the Protected by the Damned Facebook group, where the discussions revolve around humor that's a little bit more adult.

I admit our two youngest sons played Dungeons and Dragons while in high school. I'm not sure they continue to play any games, but at least I have checked that nerd-father task off my to-do list.

I hope you have a fantastic week!

Regards,

Michael Anderle

OTHER BOOKS BY THE AUTHORS

Other Middang3ard Books

Never Split The Party (01)
Late To the Party (02)
It's My Party (03)
Blue Hell And Alien Fire (04)

Death Of An Author: A Middang3ard Novella

Dark Gate Angels

Other Books by Ramy Vance

Mortality Bites Series
Keep Evolving Series
Fatebound Series
Welcome to the Dragon Show Series

Other Books by Michael Anderle

CONNECT WITH THE AUTHORS

Connect with Ramy

Join Ramy's Newsletter to get a **FREE AUDIOBOOK!**
Join Ramy's FB Group: House of the GoneGod Damned!

Connect with Michael Anderle and sign up for his email list here:

Website: http://lmbpn.com

Email List: http://lmbpn.com/email/

Facebook:
www.facebook.com/TheKurtherianGambitBooks